POPEYE
CLIMBS A MOUNTAIN

This is my
WONDER® BOOK

. . . .

POPEYE
CLIMBS A MOUNTAIN
by Charles Spain Verral

Copyright© 1980 by King Features Features Syndicate, Inc.
Published by Price/Stern/Sloan Publishers, Inc.
410 North La Cienega Boulevard, Los Angeles, California 90048

ISBN: 0-8431-4129-8

Wonder' Books is a trademark of Price/Stern/Stern Publishers, Inc.

Wonder® Books
PRICE/STERN/SLOAN
Publishers, Inc., Los Angeles
1986

POPEYE THE SAILOR wanted to climb Mount Big Nose.

"Why, Popeye?" asked his friend Olive Oyl.

"Because," Popeye said, "I want to see what's on the other side."

So early one morning Popeye and Olive packed up the car with mountain-climbing gear.

"Go get Wimpy," Popeye said, "and tell him not to forget to bring a rope. We may need it."

Wimpy was still asleep. He was dreaming, as always, of a big, delicious hamburger.

"Come along, Wimpy," Olive said. "We're ready to leave."

"ZZZZZzzzzz," Wimpy answered.

Olive finally got Wimpy up and into the car, and off
they went to Mount Big Nose.

"I can't hear the radio, Olive," Popeye complained.
"All I hear is Wimpy snoring."

"Tee-hee," Olive giggled.

At the foot of Mount Big Nose, Popeye, Wimpy, and Olive got out of the car.

"Let's start climbing," Popeye said. "I can't wait to see what's on the other side of this hill."

Wimpy yawned. "You two go ahead," he said. "I'll be along a little later. I must rest."

Popeye and Olive started up the side of the mountain.

"That Wimpy!" Popeye said. "All he thinks about is sleeping and eating hamburgers."

"Don't be a grouch," Olive said. "I'm sure Wimpy will be along later."

Popeye and Olive climbed higher and higher. And the side of the mountain got steeper and steeper.

"Blow me down!" Popeye said. "This climbing is not easy. This is hard work even for me."

"Popeye," Olive said, "I'm out of breath. I don't think I can go any higher."

Just then Olive stepped on a branch that was growing out of the rocky side of Mount Big Nose. It cracked right under her!

"Help, Popeye!" Olive screamed. "I'm falling!"

In a flash, Popeye reached down and grabbed Olive by the hands.

"Hold on tight, Olive!" Popeye said. "We sure could use that rope now. Blast that Wimpy!"

"I wish I'd stayed behind," Olive wailed. "I've got an awful sinking feeling."

At that moment, Wimpy wasn't thinking about mountain climbing. He was thinking about lunch. He had taken a frying pan from the car and built himself a fire. In the center of the frying pan was, of course, a delicious, thick, juicy hamburger.

"Oh, the noble hamburger!" Wimpy thought. "The prince of food!"

Wimpy didn't know that perched above him was another hamburger lover. A very hungry vulture, with a huge beak and a long neck, was drooling over the delicious smell of the cooking hamburger.

"Oh, yummy!" the vulture crooned to itself. "What a meal for my tummy! Just one swoop and it will be mine."

The vulture watched Wimpy's every move and waited for his chance. When Wimpy flipped the hamburger in the pan, the big bird swooped down with its beak wide open and snatched up the sizzling hamburger.

It had all happened in the wink of an eye. One moment, Wimpy was humming a happy little tune to himself. In the next, he was staring at an empty frying pan!

"GONE!" Wimpy said. "It's gone!"

ZIIIPPPP

"Come back, you thief!" Wimpy shouted as he caught sight of the vulture flying away. "I'll catch you, you villain! No one can steal a hamburger from Wimpy and get away with it!"

Grabbing his rope to use as a lasso, Wimpy jumped up

and ran after the hamburger thief. The vulture flew as fast as it could, but Wimpy went just as fast. Round and round the mountain they raced, higher and higher.

"You no good bunch of feathers!" Wimpy yelled. "I'll get you, even if I have to grow wings!"

All this time, Popeye was struggling to hold onto poor Olive Oyl.

"I am getting tired," Popeye said. "What I need is my spinach. If only I had some."

Suddenly Popeye saw a rope dangling near him.

"Blow me down!" he said. "It's Wimpy's rope!"

"Oh, Popeye!" Olive said. "We're saved!"

Popeye and Olive used the rope to climb to the top of
the mountain. As they pulled themselves over the top, they
saw Wimpy calmly munching on the hamburger that he had
rescued from the vulture. The vulture was out cold.

"Where have you been?" Wimpy asked.

Popeye, Olive, and Wimpy climbed down the mountain.
Then they got in the car and started for home.

All of a sudden Popeye stopped the car.

"What's wrong?" Olive asked.

"We've got to go back to the top of Mount Big Nose," Popeye said.

"But why?" Olive groaned.

"I forgot to take a look at what was on the other side."